CUMBRIA LIBRARIES

3 8003 04798 8811

KT-547-649

Once Upon a Wish

Amy Sparkes   Sara Ogilvie

RED FOX

For Merrianna, my wish
come true – A. S.
For Katie – S. O.

A percentage of author royalties is being donated to Bliss,
for babies born too soon, too small, too sick.
(Registered charity number 1002973) www.bliss.org.uk

ONCE UPON A WISH
A RED FOX BOOK 978 1 849 41661 0
Published in Great Britain by Red Fox,
an imprint of Random House Children's Publishers UK   A Penguin Random House Company

Penguin
Random House
UK

This edition published 2016
1 3 5 7 9 10 8 6 4 2

Text copyright © Amy Sparkes, 2016   Illustrations copyright © Sara Ogilvie, 2016
The right of Amy Sparkes and Sara Ogilvie to be identified as the author and illustrator of this work
has been asserted in accordance with the Copyright, Designs and Patents Act 1988.

All rights reserved. No part of this publication may be reproduced, stored in a retrieval system, or transmitted in any form or
by any means, electronic, mechanical, photocopying, recording or otherwise, without the prior permission of the publishers.

Red Fox Books are published by Random House Children's Publishers UK, 61–63 Uxbridge Road, London W5 5SA
www.randomhousechildrens.co.uk   www.randomhouse.co.uk
Addresses for companies within The Random House Group Limited can be found at: www.randomhouse.co.uk/offices.htm
THE RANDOM HOUSE GROUP Limited Reg. No. 954009
A CIP catalogue record for this book is available from the British Library.
Printed in China

FSC
www.fsc.org
MIX
Paper from
responsible sources
FSC® C018179

Penguin Random House is committed to a sustainable future for our business, our readers
and our planet. This book is made from Forest Stewardship Council® certified paper.

Deep in the heart of the Forest of Dreams,
a giant old oak tree is *not* all it seems.

Inside is a **secret** and **wonderful** lair,
and if you look closely, you'll see who lives there . . .

A marvellous,
magical wishgiver boy,
who works to grant wishes
and bring others **joy**.

With lotions and potions and bottles and jars,
he conjures up wish magic under the stars.

At nightfall a new wish floats in on the b r e e z e · · ·

I WISH FOR A PET

and stops at the
wishgiver's home
in the trees.

The boy gives a wink. "I know *just* the one!
Oh, this little girl will have **wonderful fun**."

So he sprinkles some dragon scales into his pot –
the water's soon bubbling, **sizzling hot**.
In go some toadstools, an acorn or two,
toenail of goblin, some old nettle stew.

The bottle is filled in the blink of an eye . . .

Then, puffing and panting, he **rows** through the sky.

He finds the right window
and says with a grin,
"I'm the wishgiver boy!
Please let me come in.
The wish that you made
is about to come **true!**"

A wish
bubble grows
for a moment
or two . . .

Then **POP!** goes the bubble. "Yippee!" the girl cries,
as a dragon appears right in front of her eyes.

Her pet is **fantastic** –
the girl jumps for joy,

and forgets all about
the wishgiver boy.

The wishgiver puffs as, with all of his might,
he rows his way home through the dark, starry night.

"It's a shame," says the boy, "that I live on my own.
How **I** wish for a **pet**, then I'd not be alone."

He closes his eyes and he stirs up the brew.
He makes a **big** wish . . .

But it doesn't come true.

In no time a new wish floats in on the b r e e z e . . .

I WISH FOR A FRIEND

and stops at the wishgiver's home in the trees.

So he reaches for moondrops
and empties the jar,

adds cloudberry juice

and sparkle of star.

The bottle is
filled in the blink
of an eye . . .

Then he rows once again through the starry night sky.

At the window he stops and says, "Open your eyes!
I've brought you a marvellous midnight surprise!
The wish that you made is about to come **true!**"

A wish
bubble grows
for a moment
or two . . .

Then **POP!** goes the bubble. The boy gives a **cheer**

as a friend and a magical banquet appear.

They sit and they gobble
with greatest **delight**,

while the wishgiver quietly slips out of sight.

All on his own, with a tear in his eye,
the wishgiver rows his way home
through the sky.

"It's a shame," says the boy, "that I sometimes feel sad.
How **I** wish for a **friend**, then I'd not feel so bad."

He closes his eyes and
he stirs up the brew.

He whispers a wish . . .

But it doesn't
come true.

"Have I missed something out?" says the boy, feeling glum.

But he jumps to his feet
as he sees a wish come.

He sprinkles in feathers,

a snippet of fur –

. . . it **sparks**
and it **flashes**,
he gives it a stir.

The bottle is filled in the blink of an eye . . .
Then he climbs in his boat and rows through the sky.

He pulls up his boat by the window and sighs,
"I'm the wishgiver boy – please open your eyes.
The wish that you made is about to come true!"

A wish
bubble grows
for a moment
or two . . .

Then **POP!** goes the bubble. The girl, in delight
whoops as she swoops on her very first flight.

As the wishgiver watches, he can't help but smile
and he tries to forget he must leave in a while.

But wishes are waiting and time's ticking on –
"Besides," thinks the boy, "she won't notice I've gone."

The girl floats around and she giggles with joy . . .

Thank you she says to the wishgiver boy.

"No one's thanked me before," thinks the boy in his boat,
as into his bottle the **magic words** float . . .

"Don't go," says the girl.
"Let's have fun – stop and play!"

The boy shakes his head. "I must be on my way.
I have wishes to grant," he says with a sigh,
and with a sad smile he bids her goodbye.

"It's a shame," thinks the boy, as he puffs through the sky,
"This rowing is hard. How I wish **I** could fly!"

The wishgiver sits all alone in his tree.
"Oh why don't my wishes work? What could it be?"
He looks at the bottle – and thinks of the girl.
Her words warm his heart as they twirl and they swirl.

Was *this* the ingredient missing before?
He opens the bottle,
daring to pour . . .

He whispers three wishes
and stirs up
the brew . . .

He takes a deep breath . . .

And his wishes come true!

Now the wishgiver flies, has a pet **and** a friend.
(Her magic words brought his bad luck to an end!)

They always remember to make time for fun.
The boy's never lonely – his sad days are done.

I WISH FOR

But while others have wishes, there's still work to do . . .

Perhaps he might even grant wishes for you!